Story Path

Madalena Matoso

How to Use Story Path

Story Path is a special kind of story – one where YOU get to choose who you meet, where you go and what you do.

It's easy...

* just decide which path you'd like to follow
* describe what you see
* then follow the path on to the next page

Want to ride an elephant through an enchanted forest, battle a troll or dress up like a princess? Fancy meeting a spooky cat, or turning a hairy monster into a teapot? Anything is possible with Story Path!

Are you ready? Then turn the page...

...and let's begin!

Once upon a time

there lived a...

this way

↑ this way

this way

Who did you choose?

* What was their name?
* What did they look like?
* Where did they live?

As they turned the corner

they were stopped by a mysterious...

this way

who gave them a magical...

Map

What did they choose?

this way

They reached out to touch it...

this way

Who did you choose?

* Can you describe them?
* What did they say?
* Were they friendly?

In a puff of smoke, they were magically taken to a strange new place. It was a...

this way

this way

What did you choose?

* What did it look like?
* What did it smell like?
* Who else was there?

They followed the path this way and that until they came across a...

KEEP OFF THE SAND

What did you choose?

* How big was it?
* Did it look cosy?
* Who do you think lived there?

They
knocked
on the
door
and it was
opened by
a family of
friendly...

They invited them in for a tasty meal of...

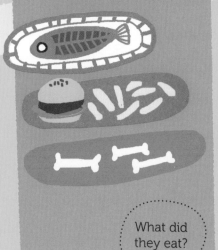

What did they eat?

Who did you choose?

* Can you describe them?
* What did they all talk about?
* What was it like inside their house?

Suddenly,
there was
a crash of
thunder!
Standing in the
doorway was a
mean and scary...

They were trapped!
But then they spied an enchanted...

which turned the monster into a...

this way

this way

What did you choose?

* What did the monster say?

* Was it funny?

* How long would the magic last?

As they made their escape,

they discovered a room full of clothes. They quickly disguised themselves as a…

this way

Then they put on a...

Which one did they choose?

this way

What did you choose?

* What colour was the outfit?
* Did it fit?
* Did anyone see them?

They crept into the next room where they stumbled upon a...

this way

this way

Which one did you choose?

* How heavy was it?
* What was inside?
* What was the best treasure?

With their pockets full of treasure they ran outside, where they found a...

They sped off as fast as lightning. Along the way they saw...

this way

this way

this way

What did you choose?

* What did it look like?
* Was it dangerous?
* What else did they see?

Finally, they made it home.

They told their friends all about their adventure and then they...

before falling asleep in their...

this way

this way

What did you choose?

* Was it comfy?

* How long did they sleep for?

* What did they dream about?

...and they lived
happily ever after.

The
End

to be continued...

BIG PICTURE PRESS

First published in the UK in 2016 by Big Picture Press,
part of the Bonnier Publishing Group,
The Plaza, 535 King's Road, London, SW10 0SZ
www.bigpicturepress.net
www.bonnierpublishing.com

Illustration copyright © 2016 by Madalena Matoso
Text and design copyright © 2016 by The Templar Company Limited

1 3 5 7 9 10 8 6 4 2
0516 008

ISBN 978-1-78370-447-7

This book was typeset in Brown Pro and Museo
The illustrations were created with pen
and ink and coloured digitally

Concept and design by Kim Hankinson
Written and edited by Kate Baker
Printed in China